THE DEVIL YOU REAP

Fear the Reaper Book 4

Written by Stacey Rourke

In this novella you will see a mention of A-hole the cat's backstory. To read the entire adventure, check out The Monster Ball Year 3!

https://tinyurl.com/yx9ao7gm

Chapter One

"You and I have some matters to discuss."

The instant the words left Lucifer's lips I called my scythe to my outstretched hand. "No," I countered, venom dripping from my tone. "I really don't think we do."

"What you saw wasn't what you think." As Luce reached for my wrist, I jerked away from his touch.

"Wasn't it? Because it looked like you killed a child to add another soul to your collection." I spat the words at him, my fingers curled into a white-knuckled fist around the staff of my scythe. "How many more do you need to complete your grimoire?"

Mouth falling open, he winced.

Fueled by his shock, I jabbed my dagger of accusation in deeper. "That's right; I know all about that. You want to turn this into a confessional? How about you tell me what's going to happen when you acquire all seventy-two souls, and how it justifies taking innocent lives?"

Lucifer's jaw tensed, his nostrils flaring. "Sacrifices had to be made, but if you would just listen—" Taking a step forward, he reached for me once more.

With a swing of my arm I positioned the hook of my weapon between us and forced my next words through tightly gritted teeth. "Explain it to me. Justify why you painted your soul with their blood, because right now I'm not seeing that as anything but monstrous."

"Everything I do is for *us*, Nyx. You know that." Risking a step closer, his chest rose and fell in agitated heaves.

"No. I don't." Behind my eyes, the scene played on repeat of him taking the life of the Duchess Anastasia, hidden behind a golden mask... But now I saw through the cracks in that façade. "I don't know anything about you. Not anymore."

"You do!" he screamed, his face reddening as the tendons of his neck bulged. "No one else in this sorry existence does, but you *do*. I need you to listen. *Please*. I can make you understand!"

The walls around us shook as the door of my apartment exploded inward with enough force to snap the jab hinge in two.

Wings stretched in a wide arch behind him, Ezekiel planted himself in the doorframe and locked stares with Lucifer. "I think she's done listening to you."

Rolling his eyes, Luce's shoulders sagged in annoyance. "You pick *this* moment to break our mutual vow of silence, Ezekiel? And I had become so very fond of it."

"This has nothing to do with you. I'm here for her." Chest puffed with purpose, Z glanced my way with a fiery intensity that made the breath catch in my throat. It had been so long since he freed his wings in front of me, I'd completely forgotten what a glorious sight it was.

Lucifer, on the other hand, was less than impressed and granted him only a humorless huff of laughter. "And you're, what? Here to rescue her from the clutches of her oldest and dearest friend?"

Z's stare flicked in Luce's direction, one brow lifting in challenge. "You're taking some grand liberties using the word *friend*. Especially since anyone who truly understands her knows she doesn't need rescuing. Ever." Turning his attention my way once more, the muscles of Z's bare chest flexed as he offered me his hand. "Jophiel gave me your message. Whatever you need, I'm here."

"What I need now is to get out of here." Moving past Luce, I purposely bumped his shoulder with mine.

He used the opportunity to catch hold of my arm and yank me to his side. "I'm begging you, Selaphiel."

Peering up at him, my eyes narrowed as if contemplating the intricacies of a work of art. "Look at that stare. So pleadingly desperate. But is any of it authentic?

How can I believe one word that comes out of your mouth when *everything* you've ever said to me has been a lie?"

His grip loosened and his voice dropped to an urgent whisper. "Please don't do this. Let me explain. Nothing I've done or accomplished will mean anything if you're not by my side."

I glanced at his hand on my arm, the implications of his touch scalding into me. "You say I know you?" I rasped. "The Lucifer I thought I knew would let me walk out of here if that's what I needed... and it is."

Fingers releasing their hold, he raised both hands beside his head and took a wide step back. "If that's what you want. But you need to know you're making a mistake."

"Then it's mine to make. You and I will have words about this matter, Lucifer. Many of them, and at great length. But it will be on *my* terms. Not you cornering me in my own apartment to force your twisted agenda." I saw the anguish my words caused, and for a moment—a brief and fleeting instant—I felt a genuine pang of regret. Then, I remembered watching Rasputin slip in Anastasia's pooling blood as he rose before his new liege, and the feeling was replaced by stone-cold resolve. "Now, I'm going to walk out of here. When I get back, you won't be in my apartment anymore. Furthermore, you will give me space until *I* decide I'm ready to talk. Are we understood?"

"Nyx, we don't have much time—" The words died on his tongue as he watched fires of rage barely held in check ignite behind my eyes. "But, of course, I will honor your wishes. I look forward to us being able to calmly discuss this... alone." He tossed a pointed glare in Ezekiel's direction.

Stretching his feathered appendages out with a roll of his shoulders, Z hooked his thumbs in the front pockets of his jeans. "I will be *wherever* Selaphiel desires me to be from this moment on."

Marching toward the door with determined strides, I hooked my arm with Z's and dragged him along behind me. "Can it. Both of you. What I want now is distance, not to listen to your pissing contest. Lucifer, you can see yourself out. Just prop the damned door up behind you so the cat doesn't get out."

Out in the hall, I let go of Ezekiel's arm and bolted down the stairs without the foggiest idea where I was going.

"Selaphiel, wait!" Retracting his wings, Z jogged to keep up. As he closed the gap between us, he pulled a V-neck, grey T-shirt from his back pocket and tugged it over his head. "Where are you going?"

My heart hammered against my ribs. The walls of Death and Taxes felt like they were closing in from all sides. "I don't know. Somewhere. Anywhere. Just not... here."

His head dipped in a brief nod, causing one rogue lock of raven hair to fall forward and tangle with his lashes. "You've got it. Come with me."

Chapter Two

Balls cracked with pins. Jovial shouts rose up from drunken patrons. Adjusting my position on the cracked vinyl barstool, I searched for some level of comfort. "I realize I said I was willing to go anywhere, but I do feel the need to point out that you have wings... and this bowling alley smells like stale cigarette smoke and plastic cheese."

"That would be from top-notch nachos here at Alley Cats. Their secret is to pile on enough meat and processed cheese that by the time you actually reach the chips, you're too bloated and uncomfortable to realize they're stale. Plus, I had a reason for bringing you here. It's literally the last place on Earth Lucifer would think to look for you." Even as

Ezekiel spoke, he kept his stare focused on a young couple teaching their toddler the intricacies of bumper bowling.

Clearing my throat, I decided to point out the first— of many—elephants in the room. "You spoke to Lucifer... for the first time in centuries. That seems like a matter worth discussing. What popped the cork from that conversational spigot?"

Chewing on the inside of his cheek, Z's gaze flicked my way. "You found out the truth."

That was a juicy enough nugget to make my brows dip in a deep V of confusion. "Beg your pardon?"

Ezekiel's fingers fiddled with a sugar packet from the center of the table, rolling and unrolling the edge of the wrapper as he chose his words carefully. "Father bound my tongue. I wasn't allowed to speak an ill word about Lucifer until you uncovered the truth for yourself."

I blinked once... and again. A fury of red-hot rage tinged the corners of my vision. "You... *knew*? All he was doing, the lives that he took, and you *did nothing to stop it*?"

Spine straightening, Z's eyes widened to saucers as he adamantly shook his head. "No! Absolutely not. I was never aware he took a life. If I had, I would have found some way to intercede. But Father... He knew souls were not being harvested as intended from the first time one failed to cross over—"

"Shortly around nineteen-sixteen," I interjected, recalling how Ezekiel bristled at Lucifer's name when I traveled back to St. Petersburg.

Jaw swinging slack, Z paused for a moment as his mind ticked back, doing the mental math. "Yeah, that's about right. Father told me the souls were being reaped and then vanishing. That's when Lucifer's little performances began. I can't say for sure; maybe it really is excruciating for him to hold the souls within him instead of allowing them to pass through. My opinion on the matter has always been that he plays it up to distract you from the actual transference process. Maybe that's just my own jaded viewpoint, but from where I stood behind the bar, I saw no redeeming qualities to vindicate him. He lied. He schemed. He bedded a *magnitude* of women. I mean, seriously, the numbers alone were staggering. Don't get me wrong, I'm not a prude. I understand you had your share of partners, too. Hell, you had your share plus a *lot* of people's share of conquests—"

Lips twisted to the side, I hitched one brow his way. "I think we're getting off topic, wouldn't you say?"

Dropping the sugar packet onto the table, Z brushed off his hands. "My point is, not only did I have no idea what he was doing with the souls, but I also hated how he treated you. Since I couldn't warn you of any of it, it was easier for my sanity to avoid him and keep the words exchanged between us to a minimum. Thankfully, you know the truth now. Which means I'm finally free to say what an absolute asshat I think the guy is, and to help you figure out what he's been plotting. Jophiel said you're in possession of some sort of grimoire that belongs to him?"

I bounced my straw up and down in the ice water I'd ordered. "Yeah, I'm glad she gave you my message. I didn't think she would. She was spouting off some shit about you being reassigned at Father's command."

A beat of awkwardly heavy silence, then… "It wasn't Father's idea. It was mine."

With so much information flying in fast and furious, I could only blink in his direction for a beat in my struggle to process it all. "You? Why?"

Planting one hand on the back of his bar stool, he shifted in his seat. "Do you remember what you said to me in the in-between?"

Unsure which nugget of wisdom he was referring to, I rattled off those that came to mind. "Stop screaming? You have to believe you can stand on top of the fog or you'll spiral into the abyss and never stop falling? Here, hide under my shroud?"

"Proud moments for me, all of them." He rolled his eyes at the memory of his panicked antics. "Nice to know you won't be forgetting them any time soon. I actually meant right before we left, when you said you couldn't guarantee where I would end up, but that wherever my heart considered home, that's where I'd find myself."

"Not an exact science to it." I shrugged, seeing little weight in my words. "We've moved around so much, it usually takes me back to the last place I was comfortable at long enough to consider home. If we moved recently, I'd go back to the previous place. That's made for some insanely weird situations. The last one I was just trying to get out the door, but the new resident insisted on showing me the Halloween costumes for all twenty of her cats."

Pressing his lips into a thin line, Z rested his elbows on the table and covered his mouth with one hand. "That's... not how I interpreted that."

I rolled my wrist, encouraging him to go on. "Talk me through it."

A rosy blush seeped up Z's neck to the tips of his ears. "It's kind of embarrassing. I'd rather not say."

Grinding my teeth to the point of pain, I fought the urge to pull my scythe from under the table and thunk him with the staff end of it. "I just found out Lucifer has been lying to me for centuries. If it's all the same to you, I'd prefer we agree to a brutal honesty policy, no matter what, from this point on. With that in mind, spill it."

Wetting his lips, Ezekiel hunted for the words that seemed lodged in his throat. "When we were in the in-between... I kissed you."

I scooted to the edge of my bar stool to allow a stumbling couple, locked in each other's embrace, room to sway their way to the bar in search of another round they most definitely didn't need. "I remember it as more of a mutual swapping of spit. But yes, I do remember the incident to which you are referring."

"You said when we left we would be transported to wherever we felt at home. And," pausing, he wiped his sweaty palms on the front of his jeans, "I ended up right outside your apartment door."

As if he had just dropped some enormous bombshell, he stopped talking and glanced my way in anticipation of my response.

"I feel there is a crucial piece of this puzzle I'm missing." Leaning forward, I took a sip from my straw. "It makes sense you would end up there. Death and Taxes has been your home, in one form or another, for a few thousand years now."

Chin falling to his chest, he rubbed a hand over the back of his neck. "I understood being in the bar. That made sense. But being outside your door—so close, yet somehow still worlds away—seemed to speak directly to our situation."

I shook my head, drying my lips on the back of my hand. "Is this because Luce and I have apartments and you have that glorified closet in the back room behind the bar? I've told you no less than a million times that I would switch with you. I can't promise your liquor supply won't get ravaged during the night, but at least you wouldn't have to sleep with bulk orders of olives and lemons over your head anymore."

"First," his eyebrows raised to his hairline as he held up one finger, "with the way you drink, you would bankrupt the bar in a week. Second, I didn't mean the apartment. I meant… between you and me. You want honesty, Selaphiel? Here you go. I've wanted to be with you since before you lost your wings. There, I said it. But there was always something in the way. Our callings. Lucifer. The rage you felt after falling. One way or another, there has always been some sort of metaphorical door between us. In that moment, it became too much. Whether we were ever together or not, I couldn't watch you pine after a guy who was blatantly deceiving you any longer. I flew home and asked to be reassigned."

"This is a lot of information to take in at a place that rents shoes," I muttered, rubbing my temples with my thumbs.

Z glanced toward a team who bowled a strike with loud hoots and hollers. "Hence me wanting to keep it to myself. This new brutal honesty campaign of yours won't be without a plethora of these kind of awkward moments. There's a little something to look forward to. For now, feel free to blow past all of this. We have way bigger issues at hand. End of times, apocalyptic goings-on that makes the fact that I even brought this up seem completely ridiculous…"

Ezekiel's words trailed off, his features softening as I reached across the table and took his hand in mine. "When I went back in time, I journeyed to an era when you and I barely spoke. I was consumed by my own pain and lashed out at you every chance I could."

"That explains a sudden memory I had of you asking me not to give up on you." With his thumb, he traced small circles on the back of my hand. "It did seem out of character for a woman who threatened to impale me whenever I made direct eye contact."

"I figured it might, but I couldn't leave things the way they were then. Not when you've become the most important person in my life. And you have, Z. Death and misery has been my life for centuries. But with you by my side, even that seemed bearable. At times it has even become—dare I say it—downright enjoyable. Because of that, what you told me here deserves my full and complete attention. However, in this particular moment—"

"The fact that Lucifer could be plotting the end of the world demands that we put a pin in that particular conversation... for now." Ezekiel offered me a sweet smile I felt clear down to my toes.

I gave his hand a squeeze of comfort. "For now. The very second we avert a potential apocalypse, we will continue this long overdue conversation." I paused before adding on the necessary disclaimer, "As long as we both make it out alive."

"All the more reason for us to handle this as quickly and efficiently as we can," he seconded with a resolute nod.

"Agreed. So... any idea where we start?"

Pulling his hand back, he grimaced. "As a matter of fact, I do. There's something I need to show you, but you're really not going to want to see it."

"It doesn't have anything to do with my aforementioned fleet of sexual conquests, does it? Because that is a lineup I do *not* want to be reminded of."

"You and me both." He chuckled. "No, there is nothing loving—carnal or otherwise—about where we're going."

"Wow, sounds like a blast, then." I pantomimed enthusiasm. "A bowling alley followed by a trip into untold miseries all in the same night? I thought we agreed to wait before you started wooing me?"

Chapter Three

"All I've ever wanted is for us to be together," Lucifer purred with his lips against my ear, breathing the words into me. "This is how we make that happen. We've bent to Father's will for far too long. Now, we have the forces needed to impose our own rule. Reign beside me, Nyx." His lips trailed down my neck, teasing over my delicate flesh in a naughty prelude.

"You lied to me," I murmured, voice heady with desire. If I was truly bothered, such an emotion was not conveyed in this scene of seduction. "For centuries you've deceived me."

Cupping my ass in both hands, Lucifer pressed my body to his and ground his enthusiasm against my thigh.

"And you'll revel in punishing me time and again as we reign on high together. Open the book, my love. Read the inscription. Allow our rule to begin and a shadow of darkness to shroud the Earth."

Never would I want for such a thing. Not for an instant would I jeopardize innocent lives as he had Anastasia's... and Father only knew how many others. Yet in this warped and twisted reality, I pulled the grimoire from beneath my shroud and cracked it open.

The instant that leather-bound cover flipped back, tendrils of darkness wisped around the room. They tossed my hair back and snaked up my arms before shooting off to wait and watch from the dark corners of the in-between.

I wanted to think I would hesitate. That I would choke on the words and be unable to utter them, knowing the harm they would cause. But I didn't. I let the incantation tumble from my lips with a devil may care nonchalance. "Notum sit porta patebit regnum caelorum. Patitur angeli, qui concussit *regna, sicuit in forti throni est minati. Nec requies animae aurora novi."*

I knew what the sentiment meant, and it filled me with icy terror. I wanted to stop it. To slam the book shut or knock it from my own hands. However, I was not cast in a starring role in this nightmarish scene. Powerlessly, I watched as my eyes blinked into ominous black voids. Darkness coated my hair, replacing my brilliant blue hue with the shade of a moonless midnight. Even Lucifer stumbled back, punched to his knees by the malicious power emanating off of me. An army of souls—all those Lucifer had gathered—materialized behind me. Seventy-two of them, falling into a battle-ready formation... behind me.

Lucifer threw his arms out wide and peered up at me as if seeing his own personal messiah.

"I knew it." His voice cracked with emotion, eyes welling with pride. "I always knew it. Nobody can match your power. It always had to be you, Nyx. I will gladly follow you, from now until the end of days. We will storm the gates of

Heaven and take what is rightfully ours by violent force. Then, you and I will usher in a new age of angels and mortals living side-by-side, ruled only by their own free will and not divine intervention."

"There will be intervention." As the words left my lips, they resonated through the in-between in a haunting echo. "My intervention."

From that empty oasis, a landscape churned and formed in the distance. One of a steep, rocky ascent that led up the mountain of truth. High atop it, the gate of Heaven sat vulnerable and exposed... mine for the taking.

I didn't look back.

Didn't contemplate the ramifications.

With resolute strides I marched toward my target. Lucifer fell into step beside me, our army of stolen souls flanking us. The beginning of the end had come... and I unleashed it.

I shoved myself away from Ezekiel, only to have him catch me and hold me upright until I could reclaim my unsteady footing.

"What the hell was that?" I gasped, sweat streaking down the middle of my back in torrents.

From where we stood outside the bowling alley, Z offered a tight smile to a concerned onlooker. "She's fine. Low blood sugar. But thank you."

The man gave a nod and walked on.

Dropping his voice to a whisper, Z glanced around to make sure no prying ears were listening. "*That* is what's going to happen if we don't find a way to prevent it. Father granted me the gift of sight in this lone instance to help battle back the darkness rising."

"You mean me. To battle against *me*!" Shaking off his hold, I paced the patch of cracked sidewalk in front of him. "How could that happen? I'm standing here, knee deep in the good fight *just as I've been doing for centuries*. What could possibly change things in such a monumental way?"

Shoving his hands into his pockets, Z's stare fell to the toes of his work boots. "When all seventy-two souls have been collected, the grimoire will tap into the darkness of the person in possession of it. That being you, it will corrupt your mind and mute any merciful thoughts you might have."

Arms falling slack at my sides, my shoulders sank. "They should really put that warning on the cover."

"It doesn't have to go down like this." Z glanced up at me from under his lush lashes. "There is another way."

"Burn the book and hop the next flight to Maui?"

That earned a mildly entertained snort of laughter. "Not quite. It'll take a little more work than that. You've made claims that you've forgiven yourself for the sins of your past. Now, you need to do it for real." From his pocket he pulled a silver ring molded into the shape of two broken wings. "Your next mission... is you. With this, we can travel back to the moment you consider to be your very worst. The one that still haunts you."

"Sounds like a fun trip."

"No, it won't be. However, by facing this troubled version of you, you can offer forgiveness and free yourself from the self-loathing that will manifest into the nightmare scenario I showed you." He started to offer me the ring, then hesitated and pulled his arm back. "Oh, and one more thing. No matter how nasty Past You gets, you can't kill her or you'll die, too."

"Well, now it just seems like you're tying my hands," I playfully jabbed, then called my scythe from its resting spot on the ground into my hand with a roll of my fingers. "I forgive myself and then what? The grimoire will only make me pissy and not murderous?"

"The inscription will change, reflected by the peace of your soul."

"Any way we can check that before the moment of truth is at hand?"

"Nope."

"This is one of those blind faith moments?"

"Yep."

"Fan-fucking-tastic."

After sliding the ring on my finger, I took Ezekiel's hand in mine. Filling my lungs to capacity, I delivered two sharp stamps of my staff and watched the world swirl around us as I prepared to meet the very worst version of myself.

Chapter Four

"Ah, fuck." One look around and I immediately knew where I was. This was definitely *not* something I was thrilled to relive in front of Z.

Spinning in a slow circle, Ezekiel glanced up at the soaring cathedral ceilings with inlayed stained glass depicting various biblical scenes. "Is this a monastery? What were you doing in a monastery?"

Planting my staff against the slate floor, I shifted my weight to lean against it. "Listen, you said it yourself, this is what I deemed to be my most awful moment. It's safe to say nothing you see here is going to be pleasant. That said, if you're going to be here, I'm going to need you to keep the questions and judgments to a minimum. I have to forgive myself for what happened, and I can't do that if I'm worried about what you're thinking."

Ezekiel pantomimed locking his lips and throwing away the key. "Judgment free zone. You do whatever it takes to move past whatever horrible torture you unleashed on these peaceful men of God."

Lips screwing to the side, I shriveled him with a glare. "Really? Now does *that* seem judgement free to you?"

"Nope, that was just for fun. I'm done now. Promise." Holding his hands up, palms out, he halted further digs—even though his impish grin made it obvious he had a few more locked and loaded.

I had one brow raised and was anticipating his next jab when footfalls echoed through the hall, growing louder as they neared. "The rules to these little jaunts have changed lately. What's the deal here? Are the people going to be able to see me or not?"

As the version of me from this time period blew in like a force of nature, all humor vanished from Ezekiel's face.

Lacing his fingers in front of him, he edged closer to offer me the solidarity of simple nearness. "She will see you when you're ready for her to see you."

"That's not at all confusing," I grumbled under my breath as my past strode in with glamourous flare.

She was stunning. A vision of sensual darkness. The gown shimmering over her curves was comprised of airy black fabric with layers of silver tulle beneath. As she moved, the two fashion elements played off each other to give an illusion similar to clouds moving across a brilliant full moon. A regal collar adorned with jewels framed her neck before the neckline plunged low between her breasts. Her hair was darker than my current hue. Glossy raven strands tipped with sapphire blue fell to her waist in thick waves.

Not two steps behind her, practically jogging to keep up, was a handsome priest with strawberry-blond hair, bright green eyes, and a smattering of freckles on the apples of his cheeks.

"Lilith, please!" he begged, his tone slathered with desperation. "I gladly broke my vows to be with you; I beg of you to allow me to stay by your side!"

Past Me spun on him, her skirt flaring out around her as she jabbed her hands onto her hips. "Someday I will learn that trysts with mortals are never worth it. You're far too clingy a species. Plus, I don't care much for the constant reminders of all you *claim* to have given up just so I would let you slide between my thighs. How can you state you've given up *anything* when you're still in this place, joining in on the ritualistic prayers to a God who isn't listening?"

The priest tried to reach for her, only for Lilith to step away. "I've been upholding my obligations only as long as we are here, my love. Yet I will give it all up to come away with you. I love you, Lilith, and I want nothing more than to spend each and every day by your side."

Knowing what was coming, I closed my eyes for a beat.

Lilith's chest swelled with a deep inhale, a cruel smile coiling at the corners of her lips. "And you're willing to forsake your Lord and savior for the chance to explore the pleasures of the flesh with me? To damn your soul for all eternity to be naked, writhing, and tangled in my attentions?"

The priest pulled back an iota, considering the ramifications of her words. "I believe God to be a loving Father who knows we can never be worthy of Him. He is well aware of what's in my heart and knows my feelings for you could never be wrong. Even leaving my life here behind, I know we will be blessed by His grace and mercy."

Letting her arms fall slack at her sides, Lilith cast her gaze skyward as a wry huff of laughter escaped her parted lips. "Is that what you think? That He's loving and kind? Sweet, foolish boy, you couldn't be more wrong. His love is conditional. And He will snatch away the warmth of His attention at your first offense and leave you wilting... alone in the darkness." Lilith inched intimately close to her priest, the curve of her breasts brushing against him and earning a throaty moan of appreciation from the visibly sweaty clergyman. "The second your lust for me consumed you, He turned his back on you. Still, you're too blind to see it. You grasp at the comfort of His fictional good graces. And *that* is why you and I can never be together."

Sniffing back a hot rush of emotion, I forced myself to face this stunted version of my former self. The Lilith days. A time in my life I tried to distance myself from in any way I could. This very day was the main reason why. Opening my mouth, I honestly couldn't say if the words that came pouring out were for Ezekiel's benefit or mine. "I was so mad at Father that I wanted to destroy the faith of any true believers. When you target another person's faith, you crush their hope. There are few things more vile than that. Still, that wasn't the worst of my sins."

If Ezekiel had an opinion on the matter, he didn't let on. Instead, he maintained his stoic silence at the scene unfolding.

The priest cupped Lilith's face between his palms, his stare pleading with her to see the truth carved on his heart. "I will do whatever it takes to be with you. Ask it, and it shall be yours. I will prove myself to you in any way I can, would you only allow me the chance."

"Mortals don't fare well when mingling with archangels," Z offered, yet still didn't pry his gaze away from Lilith. "You know that now, but it was a lesson each of us had to learn the hard way. You can't be held responsible for his actions or feelings."

"Can't I? Keep watching."

A third set of footsteps closed in, echoing all around with the finality of a coffin lid being hammered closed. Lilith glanced over the priest's shoulder—how I hated myself for not remembering his name—and gave a malicious grin at the idea that came to her.

Pushing back, she tore a cold valley of distance between her and her lover. "You speak these words as your dear monsignor approaches. However, I know this particular dance far too well. I'll spare your pride and status here by playing the part of a stranger brought here by the guilt of my own atrocious sins."

The priest's head snapped in the monsignor's direction, equal parts confusion and indecision slicing deep divots between his brows. The hands that had been clinging to her fell away, his body language cooling toward her.

I saw it there in her eyes—*my eyes*. Icy calculation. And it filled my heart with dread.

"Monsignor!" Lilith side-stepped around the enamored priest. "I'm so glad you're here. I have questions about God's plans for my life and I feel no one can help me but you."

The round-faced man, with kind eyes and an easy smile, extended his hand to her in a gracious offering. "I was coming to talk to Father Elbativeni about his duties for this evening's prayer vigil. However, such matters can wait when a soul is in turmoil. Come, my child, we will adjourn to my office to discuss all that is plaguing you."

Elbativeni. So, that was his name. No wonder I couldn't remember.

Lilith, the Lady of Lament, cozied in tight to the monsignor's side, allowing him to wrap a comforting arm around her shoulders. Then, knowing full and damned well how cruel it was, she cast a sly smile back to Father Elbativeni.

Even though I knew what was going to happen, the world slowed.

Father Elbativeni spun on his heel and seized the nearest cast iron candelabra. The pillar candles perched on it fell to the ground and rolled away as the red-faced priest charged for the monsignor with his new weapon gripped tight. Swinging the candelabra over his head, Elbativeni brought it down hard and fast. It struck the higher ranking elder in the back of the skull, blood spurting from the wound as his body crumbled to the floor. But the assault didn't stop there. Consumed by rage, the priest beat the fallen man again and again. Splashing gore painted the room and pooled on the floor beneath the slumped body.

Stunned, Lilith stumbled back, her trembling hands covering her horrorstruck expression.

"Do you see the depths of my love?" Elbativeni panted between blows. "Never again can you doubt how far I will go for you. *You are my world. You are my everything.*"

With a roll of her shaking fingers, Lilith called for her scythe. Unable to tear her wide-eyed gaze from the fallen monsignor, she floated forward on whisper-soft steps and pressed the hook of her scythe to the priest's back. His arms shot out, appendages locked stiff. As the candelabra slipped from his gore-covered fingers, his soul was sucked from his body in a series of violent twitches and bone-rattling convulsions. Only when the empty vessel of his body folded to the floor did Lilith edge closer to the frail and beaten monsignor. Crouching down beside him, she used a gentle touch and utmost care in rolling him over. Somehow, she managed to fight back a gasp at the grisly mess of battered flesh and crunched bone the quaking man had been reduced to. The sunken side of his face was all the proof she needed that his skull was cracked, his labored breathing indicating the severity of his wounds would prove fatal. Impotent to help, Lilith did the only thing she could and cradled his head in her lap as she scooted her scythe close to his side—yet kept it out of sight to avoid frightening him.

"If you have any last words, Monsignor, now would be the time." That was the first time I uttered those words. Countless times since, I'd pictured this very moment when I offered this kindness to others.

With ruby droplets spilling from his lips, the holy man battled to choke out the last sentiment of his stilling heart. "Yea... though I walk through the... valley of the shadow of death, I... will fear no evil, for You... are with me. Your... rod and Your staff, they... comfort me."

Tears slipped from Lilith's lashes unchecked, raining down on the fading monsignor. "Even after this, you turn to

Him with love and hope?" she asked, not in anger or judgment, but with genuine confusion laced with sorrow.

At the question, his bruised and swollen features softened, a sense of peace erasing his pain. "Now more than ever, my child."

As his eyes slid closed, Lilith laid the hook of her scythe to him and guided his soul toward whatever awaited him in the beyond. Task of mercy complete, she lowered his head to the ground and rose to her feet to gaze upon the death and carnage she delivered to the house of God.

"This was the last day I ever allowed anyone to call me Lilith," I croaked, pausing to wet my suddenly parched lips. "I had to distance myself from her after this. She... No, damn it, I'm here to forgive myself and that needs to start now. *I* played a sick game for my own delights and it ended with the senseless death of an innocent soul. I'm sure in Father's eyes, me allowing Lucifer to fall was the greatest of all my sins. But I've never seen it that way. *That* I did out of love. I wanted him to be happy, even if it wasn't with me.

This? This I did just to see what would happen, how far I could push one of these little starstruck pawns." Dropping my chin to my chest, I shook my head. "I never expected it to go like this."

"Did you take pleasure that it did?" Z inquired, not in judgment but genuine inquiry.

"No. Not for an instant."

Ezekiel nodded, as if I confirmed what he already knew. Reaching over without saying a word, he closed his hand around the staff of my scythe and plucked the sickle from the back of my belt. "When you step forward from where you're standing, she'll be able to see you. The only weapon you're allowed to face her with is your own faith. Faith that things will get better. Faith that she's not broken beyond repair. Faith that only *you* can offer." Moving both weapons to his opposite hand, Ezekiel's fingers laced with mine and gave a brief squeeze of support. "Remember, you're not alone in this, Selaphiel. You never were. Hold tight to that truth and you'll know exactly what you need to do. Are you ready?"

Stretching my neck in one direction, then the other, I limbered up for whatever was to come. "Not in the least. But when has that ever stopped me?" A quick pulse of comfort to his hand, then I let my fingers slip from his and took that pivotal step forward.

Chapter Five

What do you say when no words can reach a person's level of despair?

What sentiment can cut through the fog of self-loathing to reach the soul lost beneath?

It would take a being far wiser than me to know.

Accepting my own inadequacy, I settled for the simple approach. "Hello, Selaphiel."

Lilith's head snapped in my direction, her top lip curling back in a vicious snarl. "I don't know what I loathe more; being called by that name, or knowing Father had the gall to send someone to kill me whilst wearing my own face."

Holding my arms out at my sides, I let her see that I came empty-handed. "I have no weapon, and no intention of hurting you."

"Don't think that means I will show you the same kindness." Her attempt at a threat was cut off by her tripping over the body at her feet. Sucking air through her teeth, she cringed at the agonizing nightmare splattered all around.

I didn't attempt a step closer but kept my hands visible and raised. "I know what you're feeling. That stab of guilt over the monsignor. I'm not going to tell you it wasn't your fault, because we both understand the hold you possess over mortals. But I will say this: you had no way to know. What happened here? You couldn't have known it was coming. No one could."

Hand curling into a white-knuckled fist around the staff of her scythe, Lilith's desire to rip me apart wafted off her in palpable waves of malicious loathing. Not that I blamed her. I was tearing her fresh wound open further before it had even a moment to heal.

Still, the poignancy of my words earned me a momentary reprieve. "Who are you?"

Dragging my fingers through my hair, I searched my mind for some clever explanation of a situation even I didn't completely comprehend. "I'm a version of you here to offer something you need more than anything else right now."

Lilith hitched one brow at the gore painting the floor. "An armload of towels?"

"Huh," I mumbled under my breath. "So this is when I started using humor as a defense mechanism. Interesting."

"Do you have a reason for being here?" Lilith snipped. "Otherwise, be gone. As you can see, I'm a bit busy at the moment."

"And you will be for centuries to come." Head tilted, I offered her a compassionate smile. "For countless lifetimes you will work tirelessly to earn your redemption, convinced it's Father's forgiveness you need. But it's not. It hasn't been since this precise moment. The real person you've been paying penance to... is you."

"That's... deep. Really, some insightful... stuff." Lilith peered at the mess around her, then back at me. "And that message of hope would probably be better received if I wasn't currently surrounded by carnage."

My mouth opened to argue, only to realize there was no counterpoint to make. "And yet, this is the exact moment you need to hear it."

Chewing on the inside of her cheek, she battled back a hot rush of tears. "How is it you plan to impart such optimism when you're still here, walking this earth, the same as me? Where is the upside of knowing that," she waved her hand up and down in front of me, gesturing to my appearance, "what appears to be *eons* from now—"

"Alright," I interjected, talking over her, "we age slowly and you know it. At most, I look like your slightly older sister."

"*Millenniums* from now," she corrected in full vindictive spite, "I will still be stuck here, in this same nightmarish wasteland, helping souls move on when I can't?" As she closed the distance between us, I could see that the monsignor's blood had mingled with her tears, streaking her face with trails of pink. "How can I hold on to any hope when I look at you and know there is no escape for me? I'm a prisoner now and will be for any kind of foreseeable future. So, what does it matter? Whether I feel Father doesn't forgive me, or I don't forgive myself, it changes nothing. Who the warden is doesn't change the strength of the bars."

I could feel her pain, and not just by memory. Sorrow radiated off of her in heady waves that threatened to drag me under and sink me to the depths alongside her. She needed a lifeline, some element of mercy, and I was living proof one hadn't come.

Yet.

Risking life and limb, I placed my hands gently on her upper arms and pulled her into a loving embrace. I wanted to take the pain from her. To heal her battered heart and erase the years of suffering I knew laid ahead of her.

She did not appreciate the sentiment and bristled at the contact. "What the fuck are you doing?"

Clearing my throat, I pulled back out of range of the scythe gripped tightly in her fist. "Sorry, got caught up in the moment and forgot we don't like people. Or to be touched. Or to be touched by people."

Lilith took a step back and then another, casting herself back into the shadows of the gory scene she had brought down upon the monastery. "Look, I get what you're trying to do. I have no doubt this particular night probably left scars I can never recover from. Even so, there is nothing you can say that will make this better. No words can wash away the blood that now stains my soul. There is no forgiveness on Earth or in Heaven for a sin this dastardly. Even though I didn't wield the weapon, it was *my* influence that motivated its fatal swings."

She was right. There were no words. What she needed was an undeniable symbol of hope... and forgiveness.

I could only think of one thing that could convey that message.

Stepping back, I squared my shoulders. Ezekiel stated I would only be armed with my faith. While that wasn't a muscle I had flexed in a while, I was prepared to strain a few things using it now.

"You're absolutely right. You don't need words. You need to see... *this*." Closing my eyes, I rolled my shoulders and prayed for the impossible.

Nothing.

Not one damned thing happened.

"Uh... what am I looking at? Do you have a cramp? Feeling gassy?" Annoyed to have to ask that question, Lilith clucked her tongue against the roof of her mouth. "While I appreciate whatever the hell it is you're trying to do, I'm kind of in the middle of something. Any of the other priests could walk in at any moment and—"

"Oh, shut it. You know you're going to skirt out of here before you have to answer any questions. You knew that the second the monsignor drew his last breath. Now zip it so I can concentrate." Brushing off her interruption, I shook out my arms and legs and tried again.

It had been so long and was an unbelievable longshot.

A pure Hail Mary attempt.

But this was going to work.

It had to.

A deep breath.

A silent prayer.

… and a purposeful roll of my shoulders.

Before my eyes opened, I knew they were there. A gust of wind tossed my hair over my shoulders. Blissful weight pulled at my shoulder blades. A sharp snap cracked behind me, followed by an awestruck gasp.

Raising my chin from my chest, I blinked back the tears of happiness burning behind my eyes and offered Lilith a beaming smile. "Heaven hasn't given up on you, Selaphiel. So don't give up on yourself."

Lilith stumbled forward. One step, then another, before falling to her knees before me. "My wings. I... get my wings back."

I felt her lightness in my own heart, the weight of guilt lifting.

Crawling closer, she scrambled to catch hold of my hand. "When does it happen? How? Please! If you could just give me a century to aim for!"

Afraid to offer up any information that could change anything, I stepped back and faded from her world.

There Ezekiel waited with a sweet schoolboy grin. "Of all the looks I've ever seen you in, this is my favorite. Selaphiel, Warrior of Heaven, Archangel of the Lord, would you fancy a flight?"

"More than anything." Laughter bubbling through my tone, I accepted my scythe when he offered it to me. "But, we came here through this, and it's the only way to get back to our time. So, we're going to venture back, crack open that grimoire, and end all this once and for all. Then, I'm taking to the sky and doing figure eights until I puke."

"Sounds like a very disgusting—yet rewarding—plan." Z chuckled and hooked his arm with mine.

"Don't worry. I've waited far too long. We *will* get our chance." Two stamps of my staff and the world warped around us.

If only I'd known nothing in it would ever be the same again …

Chapter Six

Face-to-face with my past self, wings framing me and the light of hope burning brightly behind my eyes, it was easy to feel confident and victorious in the moment.

But that was then.

Hunkering in the back alley behind Death and Taxes with the grimoire hugged tight to my chest and the knowledge of the literal hell I could unleash in the forefront of my mind, was entirely another matter. "And we're sure I *completely* forgave myself? No hidden darkness marring my heart that might send an army of evil charging the pearly gates? Because I can think of tons of other bad shit I've done that I haven't even touched on yet. Like this one time, I went to a Doors concert in Miami and convinced Jim Morrison to—"

"Selaphiel, stop," Ezekiel soothed, rubbing his hands up and down my arms. "*You* were all that was preventing you from getting your wings back. Now that you have them, you're ready. Unless... you let too much doubt in. Then, your wings will morph into inky black reptilian appendages and you'll develop a forked tongue." At my bulging eyes, he quickly backpedaled. "I'm kidding! I'm fairly certain that can't happen. Like, ninety-five percent sure. Eh, maybe seventy-thirty."

Shoulders sagging, I let the book fall farther down my torso. "You're the worst. You know that? How is sarcasm in any way helpful right now?"

"If nothing else, it made you relax a little bit." Leaning in, his silky hair tickled my forehead as he dotted a kiss to the tip of my nose. "You've got this, Sel. I promise."

Pulling the grimoire away from me, I glanced down at its leather-bound cover and traced my pinkie finger over one of the golden images carved into it. "Do we have a back-up plan in case shit goes sideways? A divine grenade we can throw to wipe out all those malicious souls?"

"We do." Z's chin dipped in a resolute nod. "It's you armed with both your weapons, and me behind you taking care of any who happen to break through."

A deep inhale through my nose, and I exhaled through pursed lips. "That is not a plan, it's a cluster fuck. Big difference."

"Po-tah-tow/poe-tay-toe." He let one shoulder rise and fall in a casual shrug.

"More like perfectly choreographed ballet/mosh pit."

One final squeeze to my upper arms, and Z took a wide step back to allow me space for whatever was to come. "It doesn't matter, because we've taken every precaution needed. Lucifer hasn't even been able to collect all seventy-two souls. That gives us an advantage. Now, you're going to open that book, read the inscription, and everything is going to be okay. There's no way this can go wrong."

My mouth swung open in shock that he would dare to jinx us in such a bold fashion. "Do you *want* a storm cloud of flying monkeys? Because talk like that is exactly how you get them."

Prying the book from my death grip, Ezekiel dusted off the cover and offered it to me once more. "Once you start reading, you can't stop, no matter what happens. Until the inscription is read in its entirety, the ball is still loose... so to speak."

"And you're going to make sure I'm allowed to finish reading... all by yourself?" I hitched one brow in doubt. "I mean, not that you aren't a badass dude, because you are. But we are talking about a slew of the nastiest souls the world has ever seen."

"Then I guess it's a good thing I have help." Taking a wide sidestep to my right, Ezekiel granted me a full view of the alley behind him.

Jophiel emerged from the shadows, armed with her flaming sword. Perched on her shoulder was A-hole. As Jo strode straight for me, my cat launched off of her and landed in a low crouch… in human form.

Her hair cascaded down her back in mahogany waves. A shift of fabric girded her breasts and pelvis, yet the rest of her voluptuous curves were on full display. Rising to her feet, she tossed me a playful wink. "It's good to see you again, Nyx. Although the circumstances are far less appealing than last time."

Last time. The night off I took, back when I was attempting to outrun my problems. Instead, I learned my cat's rather odd backstory and helped her resolve a centuries' long vendetta. "Nephthys, Egyptian Goddess of Death… who is most definitely *not* Egypt's version of a reaper."

That earned me a playful eyeroll as she clucked her tongue against the roof of her mouth. "I think we both know that's not true. However, my power *does* exceed yours.

Which is why your man-friend begged me to offer you aid. He even arranged for me to maintain my human form for an entire week as thanks. That said, we need to hurry this along. I have a list of glorious debauchery to indulge in while I'm here."

"Do we need to have the condom talk?" Perplexed by that thought, my head tilted in question. "Can cats get chlamydia?"

"I keep myself very well protected, I assure you." With a roll of her fingers, Nephthys made a bone-handled dagger appear in her hand. She flipped it over in her palm— once then again—before sliding it into the fabric tied at her hip. All the while her gaze stayed locked on Ezekiel, her tongue flicking out to moisten her full lips. "Is this the sexy bartender you were telling me about? If so, I will honor our bond by leaving him alone. If not, I fully intend to leave claw marks down his back by morning."

Trying unsuccessfully to stifle a grin, Z glanced my way. "You talked to your cat about me? *And* called me the sexy bartender?"

I silenced him with a glare. "First of all, don't pretend you've never looked in a mirror. You know what you're working with. Second, she wasn't a cat at the time. She was in this form." I waved a hand in her direction. "We bonded, and then I guarded the door while she boned a mouse-shifter. It was a big night for everyone. Can we get back to the grimoire now please?"

"Where did we land on..." Nephthys trailed off, jerking her head in Z's direction.

Pressing his lips into a thin line did not prevent Ezekiel's face from reddening as he battled back his laughter.

"*No one is leaving claw marks on anyone! Now can we please get back to stopping the damned apocalypse?*" I shrieked a few octaves louder than necessary.

Inching up alongside Nephthys, Jophiel muttered out of the corner of her mouth, "If human interactions are always this entertaining, I'm beginning to understand the appeal of Earth."

Glancing down at the slightly shorter woman, Nephthys's gaze traveled over her with piqued interest. "They aren't. Normally humans are quite dull. You're lovely, by the way. Do you have plans for after we stop the gates of Heaven from being stormed?"

Unable to form words, I hugged the grimoire to my chest and blinked in Z's direction. "Words cannot express how happy I am that you arranged for them to be here. Really, just super helpful."

"I get that was sarcasm, but I can't feel even a little bad about it. Not when it brought me such joy." The corners of Ezekiel's amber-colored eyes crinkled with his mischievous grin. "Look at their presence here as motivation to get this over with."

"Good point." Battling back the pterodactyl-sized butterflies in my gut, I cracked open the book. An ominous gust ripped from the grimoire, tossing my hair back as it swirled through the alley with the stale scent of moldy parchment. The pages flipped on their own, settling on the inscription that would prove to be a salvation... or a curse.

"Oh, look," I mused, swallowing hard around the lump of trepidation lodged in my throat, "the blinding fear is back."

Holding her sword in a two-handed grip, Jo assumed a battle-ready stance. "You read. We'll protect you."

"Protect her from what?"

I closed my eyes for a beat at the sound of Lucifer's voice, a chill racing down my spine with the awareness that our situation had just made the shift from bad to worse. Turning to face him, I said nothing but positioned myself for him to see his treasured book cradled in the bend of my arm.

I expected vengeance.

Wrath.

Blind fury that I would dare threaten the plan he spent centuries orchestrating.

Instead, a knowing smile lifted the corners of his rose petal lips. "All I've ever wanted is for us to be together. This is how we make that happen. We've bent to Father's will for far too long. Don't you see? Now, we have the forces needed to impose our own rule. Reign beside me, Nyx. Embrace your destiny as my dark queen."

Struck by a dizzying case of déjà vu from how similar his words were to the vision Ezekiel showed me, I clung tight to the differences. I had changed elements already. The end of this particular story hadn't been written... had it?

"You lied to me," I stated, not lost under his spell of seduction as I had been in Ezekiel's vision, but as a woman hurt far too many times by a man who claimed to love her. "For centuries, you've deceived me. How can I believe one word that comes out of your mouth?"

Lucifer risked a step closer, earning a cat-like hiss from Nephthys. Respecting her snarl, he stopped and held up both hands to prove he carried no weapon or ill intent. As if he would need any sort of weapon to cause unimaginable pain. His hands were empty when he carved out my heart and ground it under his heel.

Voice a soothing whisper, his stare locked with mine. "You know me, Nyx. You know who I am and how I feel about you."

"Stop saying that!" My fingers curled around the edges of the book, bending the corners with firm claws of boiling venom. "Don't for one second pretend that any amount of shared intimacy somehow justifies all the lies you told. Moments of tenderness don't erase the scheming and manipulation. If anything, they make what you've done even more cruel."

"You're right." He nodded, one lock of flaxen hair brushing his forehead with the motion. "And I am ready to spend the rest of eternity making it up to you. You've opened the book, my love. Read the inscription. You will act as the final seventy-second soul that allows us to construct the bridge home. Once we have taken the throne of Heaven, we will repair the bond between us and come out on the other side stronger than ever before."

He believed he had won. That was why he was so calm and encouraging. He was counting on my own self-loathing to be the tool needed to secure his victory. Somehow, knowing that plunged the dagger of betrayal in deeper still.

Tossing my bangs from my eyes, I squared my shoulders and met his gaze with frosty resolve. "Since the very beginning, when I opened that gate, all I ever wanted was to be enough for you. Enough to make you stay. Enough to make you loyal. Enough to earn your love. But I see the truth now, Lucifer." Tears slipped from my lashes unchecked, streaking down my face and raining down on the tips of my scuffed boots. "You want to keep me broken and damaged because it makes you feel better about the shit you've done. Unfortunately for you, I've owned my mistakes. I've forgiven myself. And I refuse to take responsibility for your actions. You took innocent lives. Not me. And it wasn't for us, or for any kind of greater good. It was to accomplish your own twisted agenda. Luckily, in the light of this grand epiphany, I came armed with a secret of my own." Turning my back to him, I snapped my wings out in an imposing canopy of truth and locked stares with Ezekiel. "Keep him back. We finish this now."

"You got your wings back? When? *How*?"

Lucifer launched forward, only to be stopped by Ezekiel planting a hand in the center of his chest. "Not another step, Lucifer."

Forcing his words through clenched teeth, Luce glared Z's way out of the corner of his eye. "Get your hand off me. It's as a courtesy to Nyx that I haven't beaten you down, but my generosity is running out."

"You think I'm intimidated by you?" Z taunted, bumping Lucifer's shoulder with his. "You're an ex-angel with daddy issues. Do your worst, pretty boy."

Who threw the first punch, I couldn't say. But it was followed by the sounds of a scuffle and Nephthys's appreciative moan. "Mmm, can we spray oil on them? That would make this show even more delectable."

"Can you focus, please?" Jophiel demanded, positioning herself between me and the brawling boys. "Selaphiel, *read*!"

Trusting they had my back, I bowed my head to the dust-covered pages. Swallowing hard, I began. "*Hic ex animis ultra constringo vos volo.*" Being fluent in Latin, I was well aware that by uttering those words I bound all the souls connected to the grimoire to my will. Which was a form of commitment I never knew to be terrified of... until that moment. "*Et ploremous ante dominum venite.*" That was me commanding them to come and kneel before their master. A suggestion I truly prayed was metaphorical.

To my great regret, that would not be the case. A heavy fog rolled in from all around, spewing forth a sea of malicious souls. Black eyes. Faces set in masks of fury. All their attention locked on me. Yep, that was it. When this was all over, I was leaving the worst book review ever for the grimoire.

Pulling her blade, Nephthys fell into a low crouch and purred her enthusiasm. "Oh, this is going to be fun."

Jophiel adjusted her footing and positioned her flaming sword up alongside her head. "We have different definitions of that word, but here we go."

The two women launched into a skilled attack to no avail. With each slice they delivered to the angry horde, the marching souls dissipated in wisps of darkness only to regenerate in their same shadowy forms. My palms itched for my weapons, fingers twitching to call for my scythe and join the fight.

Sensing my hesitation, Ezekiel spun around in the middle of driving an elbow into Lucifer's jaw and screamed my way, "Selaphiel, *read faster!*"

Glancing back to the book, my frantic eyes searched the page for where I left off. *"Animarum et corporum cinis projectus est in oculis meis ut praedicaretis tuo tandem iudicio gehennae."* Slamming the book shut, I screamed the words in English for good measure, *"Souls cast out, bodies to ash, by my command you're sentenced to hell at last!"*

Lucifer shoved Ezekiel off of him and scrambled to his feet as a desperate shout tore from his lungs. *"No!"*

The instant the words left my lips, the ambling onslaught of souls... froze. Heads falling back, their eerie frames were turned inside out as the essence they were comprised of was forced out in a gush of inky black energy. The earth shook beneath our feet, concrete splintering into a gaping maw that sucked the souls down to the depths of depravity and despair. Even the grimoire rotted in my hand, cracking into ash before disintegrating into nothingness.

Silence fell.

Chest rising and falling in agitated heaves, Lucifer peered my way with tangible hatred. "You've changed nothing," he growled, his top lip curling back from his teeth. "You believe I would hinge all my aspirations on this? Think again. All you've accomplished is ensuring that when I ascend to my throne, you won't be by my side. This is the day, Selaphiel, in which you became my enemy."

Head tilted, I considered him through narrowed eyes. "Funny, that day happened for me when I watched you stab a child."

"Then I suppose we have nothing further to discuss." Loathing coated each word he spat, yet the countless years we spent together allowed me to see past that outward mask of rage. Swirling in the depths of his boiling stare were ripples of genuine sorrow.

The twitch of his nostrils was caused by an ill-fitting mask of indifference he was trying to force into place.

That tendon bulging beneath his jawline held back words he longed to speak.

Lucifer was in pain. What he considered to be my betrayal cut him deep.

While I refused to give an inch, the high arch of my wings sank. "It's not too late, Luce. Those souls have moved on. You will answer for the lives you took, that's inevitable, but it doesn't need to escalate any further than this."

I watched as my suggestion hit him like a stab to the gut, his face crumbling from the blow. "There's no coming back from this, and you know that. My only option is to see this through. Death or freedom. One will be mine to claim before the sun rises."

"You're going to storm the gates of Heaven alone?" I asked, keeping my tone soft and measured. I prayed some ounce of clarity would break through. "How do you plan to get there? Angelic Uber?"

A sardonic grin tugged at one corner of his lips. "I've been making other arrangements." A roll of his shoulders called forth a gruesome symphony of cracking bone and flesh snapped taut. From his shoulder blades stretched a wide canopy of wings that could only be described as demonic with its patchwork quilt of stitched together carnage.

Ezekiel crossed himself.

Fingers slipping from the hilt of her sword, Jophiel fell to her knees.

Nephthys took a wide step back, jutting the point of her blade out in front of her.

My scythe was in my palm in a blink, my opposite hand reaching behind me to grab my sickle from my belt. "Lucifer, what have you done?"

Snatching Jo's flaming sword from where she lost hold of it, he lifted from the ground with one mighty flap of those gruesome appendages. The motion stirred up a dry wind that reeked of rot and decay. "What I had to," he rasped, and soared skyward.

Ezekiel's wing brushed my upper arm as he edged up beside me with his glare still locked on Luce. "The three of us with wings can hold him back long enough for those beyond the gate to prepare for battle."

A knot of unease tightened in my gut, warning me of the body count that plan would result in. Human or angel, Lucifer would spare no one. "No, I face him alone."

Ezekiel's feathers ruffled in frustration. "That's suicide, Selaphiel. Can you even fathom the darkness he had to evoke to create those leathery monstrosities? The guy is well beyond the point of being reasoned with."

Clutching both weapons low at my sides, I offered him a sad smile. "You told me I was put in this position because I'm the only one who can get through to Lucifer. It was *you* that encouraged me to have faith and believe. Now, I have to ask you to do the same. Death has been my life for far too long. If I can prevent any more blood from being spilled, that's exactly what I'm going to do."

As I uttered the words, peace washed over me, breathing into me an awareness that I was choosing the right path.

An epic battle raged across Ezekiel's features. While I'm sure he bitterly hated it to his very core, he stood down. "I don't like this. Not for a second. What the hell am I supposed to do? Wait to see if it suddenly starts raining angels?"

"You're going to handle this like you do any other mission I venture off on—trust that I've got this and sling drinks." With a jerk of my head, I gestured to our audience of two. "They could definitely use a little something to take the edge off. I would suggest top-shelf Russian whiskey for the cat, and something in the Schnapps family for the angel. And, if I can make a special request? Have a flight of rum waiting for me when I get back. One way or another, I'm going to need it."

Chapter Seven

One flap of my onyx wings, then another. Each driving me faster and farther than the one before. I rose above the clouds, guided by the ethereal light beaconing from the paradise I once called home. With my wings treading a steady pulse behind me, my feet sank into the thick, buoyant carpet of clouds. Lucifer should have beat me there, yet all I could see was a billowing sea of rolling white mist leading to the grand archway of Heaven's regal gate. How many times had I dreamt of being here? To see that gate open wide and welcome me over that marble threshold?

All those centuries, yet somehow it seemed... smaller.

"This is it, then?" Lucifer's voice came from behind me, a deep tremor of loathing and regret.

"So it would seem." Bracing myself for whatever was to come, I turned to face him and my heart shattered. His grotesque wings beat against the air, the flaming sword casting eerie shadows that sharpened his features to a deadly edge. In that instant, he looked every bit the beast history painted him as. A conniving entity capable of being a serpent of temptation. The personification of evil. The King of Hell. An ominous demon able to evoke fear in the hearts of many.

Head tilting, Lucifer glared at my wings with palpable envy. "Tell me, how did it play out when you groveled to Father and begged Him to return those? Did you prostrate yourself in desperate prayer? Sob? Plead for forgiveness? Did you promise to bring Him my head if it earned you His favor?"

"I haven't spoken to Father since the day I was banished for helping you." There was no judgment or accusation in my tone, just blatant fact. "My wings returned when I stopped hating myself. Safe to say you took a slightly different route." I jerked my chin toward his contraptions of cartilage and flesh.

"How we got here doesn't matter," Luce sniffed as if battling back his own crushing emotions. "I'm done waiting. I'm done paying penance to an entity who refuses to acknowledge I exist. One way or another, this ends today. If I have to force my way inside, so be it."

Wetting my lips, I straightened both of my arms out to the sides... and dropped my blades. They vanished into the clouds where a roll of my fingers caught them in a cradle of cumulus. "It won't be by violence at my hands."

"And that little stunt is supposed to accomplish what?" he pressed, hitching one flaxen brow. "Make me reconsider cutting you in two?"

"Giving you at least a moment's hesitation would be nice." I lifted one shoulder in a dismissive shrug. "Even so, this isn't about me. You want to be allowed back into paradise. What do you think that's going to look like if you have to torch the place to get inside?"

Flapping those ghoulish wings harder still, he floated above the clouds and loomed over me as an angel of malicious darkness. "And what would you have me do? Continue to wait, doing what we're told day after day—year after year—in hopes that someday it will be enough? No. We paid our penance time and again. How long would you allow Him to punish us?"

"As long as He wants!" I shouted back, the intensity of my tone easily surpassing his. "That's up to Him, not you. You don't get to storm in there and force His forgiveness. That's not how it works. You want to mend that shattered trust? *You fucking earn it!*"

Lucifer's face reddened, whether it was from the strain of flapping those atrocious appendages or our conversational topic, I couldn't say. "And what if it's never enough? What if all we've done has been for nothing?"

I let my hands fall to my sides with a slap and forced my tone back to something that resembled calm. "We fucked up, Luce. Both of us did. You storming the gate isn't going to change that."

Leveling the sword at my head, his top lip twitched into a snarl. "I've made my decision. Now get out of the way, Selaphiel."

I shook my head, offering him a soft smile. "I can't do that. We started this together, and we'll finish it together."

Closing the distance between us, he forced his words through gritted teeth. "I won't ask you again."

Holding his stare, I refused to back down or give an inch. "Then I'll die saving you from yourself. You wanted free will. You wanted this life. I made that happen. I followed you here. Then, instead of honoring the terms set out for us, you tried to plot and scheme your way back into Heaven. Will it be enough then? Will you finally be happy?"

Lucifer fought to keep the blade steady in his quaking arm as he battled with his conflicting emotions. "I want... this over," he spat the words with venomous fury. "I want—"

In a brazen move that shocked even me, I used the back of my hand to sweep the sword aside. "To go home," I filled in for him.

Tears of raw anguish flooded Lucifer's eyes, his posture sagging with defeat. "I know what we gave up and I want it back. The life in paradise. The love of Father... I just..." Wings failing him with both physical and emotional exhaustion, Lucifer's massive frame slumped forward. Lunging for him, I caught his trembling body as he shook with sobs that radiated out from his troubled soul. "I'm sorry, Sel. I'm so sorry."

Holding him tight, I pressed a kiss into his hairline and whispered, "You have to let go, Luce. Forgive yourself and vow to do better. That's the only way you can find peace." I curled my finger under his chin and raised his gaze to meet mine. "And I want that for you. I truly do."

Tears slipped over his cheeks, adding a touch of humanity to his otherwise unattainable perfection. "Can you ever forgive me?"

My fingertips traced over his forehead, brushing the hair back from his face. "What I think, what I feel, doesn't factor into this. If you concern yourself with that, you'll be substituting one facet that's out of your control with another. It's time to focus on looking inward and finding a way to forgive yourself."

"How?" Desperate hands gripping my arm tight, he pleaded for answers I couldn't give. "All I've done. All the blood I've spilled. How can I ever lie to myself and pretend that's okay?"

He was right. His sins would eat at him, tempting him into traps like this time and again, because they were easier than dealing with the pain.

There was no turning back.

No fresh start.

If he was ever going to earn the forgiveness from Father he craved, a meeting between the two needed to be arranged.

That was where my particular skillset came in. Gently combing my fingers through his silky hair, I breathed my words against his cheek. "If you could say anything at all to Father right now, what would it be?"

Letting the flaming sword slip from his fingers into the cradle of a cloud, Luce wrapped his arms around me and buried his face against my vest. "I'd say that I pursued what was never meant to be mine with reckless abandon. That I wish I could say if I had it all to do again, I would do things differently. But I don't know if that's true. How could I ever pretend myself capable of turning a blind eye to what became my obsession?"

Scorching tears slipping from my lashes, I rubbed his back with one hand while the other called for my scythe. I closed my eyes as the weight of the weapon settled into my palm and tried to memorize the feeling of his body against mine. "I love you, Lucifer. I need you to know that."

Acting before I could change my mind, I pressed the side of my hook against his back.

As his essence drained out in rolling tendrils of brilliant violet, Luce's sapphire stare fixed on my face. There were no traces of shock to be seen. No tremors of fear. Just a thankful smile as he welcomed his own finality.

"I love you, too." Those were the last words Lucifer spoke before the light of life faded behind his eyes and the love that once defined my existence... died.

Chapter Eight

Silence.

An agonizing hush had fallen in a reality that no longer made sense.

The world... was without Lucifer.

Drawing air into my lungs hurt.

The hole punched through my heart ached.

Turning my scythe over with trembling hands, I found a new rune burned into the blade. Wings bound by a pentagram between them. That mark was all that remained of Luce.

The gentle flap of my wings stirred up a delicate breeze that kissed away the burn of tears zigzagging over my cheeks. It was the only solace to be found in that moment of unimaginable sorrow.

That was, until a voice long denied to me spoke my name. "Selaphiel, the sacrifice you made here was a noble one. I know it wasn't easy, but I couldn't be more proud of you."

How many centuries had I ached to hear the soothing cadence of Father's voice? Yet now it ground fat granules of salt into an open and festering wound.

"I didn't do it for You," I managed, forcing the words through clenched teeth.

"I'm very well aware of that. You acted purely out of love. I can think of no kinder or more compassionate offering." Father floated closer, His brilliance casting waves of warmth over my hunched frame.

Wiping my tears away with the heel of my hand, I glanced His way and my breath caught. It had been so long, I'd forgotten how easy it was to be awestruck by the peace and clarity that emanated off of Him. We called Him Father, but that implied a gender He didn't really possess. He wasn't male nor female, young nor old, black nor white. He was a being of light and energy. Mother. Father. Life. Death. The beginning. The end. It was all in Him.

Sniffing back my emotions, I turned my staff and examined the blade that now held Lucifer's essence. "What will become of him?"

Awash with the glow of divinity, Father offered me a loving smile. "He will be reincarnated and given a second chance to be the man I know he's capable of being. Hopefully, beginning as a mortal child will provide him the tools needed not to fall victim to his own sinful jealousy."

Ice seeping into my veins, I rose to my full height with one flap of my wings. "All he wanted was to go home. To be welcomed back into Your kingdom."

Folding His hands in front of him, Father's head tilted. "You're displeased. Would you prefer I judge him now for all he has done? I fear the outcome would be far worse."

Letting my staff hang low at my side, I fought to keep my expression neutral despite my raw and warring emotions. "I would have preferred You didn't cut us off completely. That You would have offered guidance and encouragement. Maybe then Lucifer wouldn't have been driven to such desperate measures. Instead, You left us floundering alone. But that's okay. I won't repeat Your mistake. If Lucifer is being cast back down to Earth, I will be there to guide him in any way I can."

"He won't remember you, Selaphiel, or have any recollection of who he once was." Voice dropping to a soothing whisper, Father offered me His hand. "You can come home now. The gates are open and welcoming you. You have more than earned the honor. Take your place beside me and join your brothers and sisters in the kingdom of Heaven."

I stared down at His offered hand. At His beautiful coursing energy, from which all life was made... and hesitated. "I won't make light of such an invitation. There was a time when that's what I wanted more than anything else in this world. Sadly, I have to decline. For centuries, all I've had is Lucifer and Ezekiel. I won't turn my back on them now. Not to mention, I've gotten pretty good at this reaper thing. Who's going to hunt down the truly nasty souls if I don't?"

Father nodded, His extended arm sinking to his side. "And if Ezekiel decides he's ready to come home?"

Wetting my lips, I tried to deny the fist of fear that closed around my heart. "I fell from paradise in the pursuit of free will. I'd be a hypocrite if I punished him for wanting the same. My feelings for him won't change based on geography."

A parental smirk tugged at the corners of Father's lips. "And what type of feelings would those be? What are your intentions with that boy?"

Eyebrows lifting toward my hairline, I tossed Him a challenging grin. "You're an all-knowing entity. I'm fairly certain You have a few ideas."

Chapter Nine

Cloaked beneath my shroud, I entered Death and Taxes. Clinging to the shadows, I simply watched and soaked in the last few moments of normalcy before everything changed. Nephthys and Jophiel sat side-by-side at the bar, laughing so hard tears streamed down their faces.

"I mean, he was a mouse-shifter, so it makes sense. Still, it was *tragically* disappointing!" Doubled over in peals of laughter, Nephthys slapped a hand to the bar to stop herself from tumbling off her stool.

Jo couldn't speak. Face beet red, all she could do was shake her head and emit a high-pitched squeak that would make dogs cringe. But it was Ezekiel to whom my stare was drawn. Behind the bar, the muscles of his arms bulged as he scrubbed glasses with a vigor that suggested he blamed water spots for all his woes. How I would love to see him smile one more time. To have another moment of lighthearted banter that always managed to make my mess of a life seem bearable. But the news I came to deliver could kill the bond between us... forever.

Knowing I couldn't put it off indefinitely, I stepped forward and shrugged off my hood. Laughter died away. Conversation silenced. Three sets of eyes snapped in my direction, scouring over me in search of clues as to what had happened. Striding across the room—boots scuffing over the reclaimed wood floors—I said nothing but set my scythe on the bar top with a clank.

Nephthys glanced at my blade. Missing nothing, her pupils contracted to feline slits as she peered at the fresh rune carved on my hook. Clearing her throat, she slid off her bar stool and hooked her arm through Jo's. "Let's give these two some privacy to talk. Not to mention I have an experiment I want to try that involves your wings. Namely, if you flap them *really* fast, will your entire body vibrate? If so, I may have a use for that."

Jo's eyes narrowed with interest. "Does that involve carnal relations? Because, I mean, Heaven is great, but we don't do that there. I would *absolutely* be interested in seeing what the fuss is all about."

Despite my trepidation over the conversation to come, a warning siren went off in my head. "Whoa, hey!" Rising up on my tiptoes, I shouted after them as they headed up the stairs, "Use Lucifer's apartment! Do *not* have sex on my bed!"

Glancing back over her shoulder, Nephthys's nose crinkled with disdain. "In cat form you're okay with me sitting on your pillow and cleaning my nether regions for hours, but in human form I can't copulate there?"

Blinking her way, I made peace with the fact I would have to burn all of my bedding. "No. I'm actually not okay with that at all, and I feel my life was simpler when I didn't know that was happening."

With matching shrugs, the pair sauntered on.

Indifferent to my pillow plight, Z dried his hands on the towel on his shoulder with his gaze locked on my scythe. "Lucifer?"

Filling my lungs to capacity, I shook my head. "He's not in there... anymore. Father decided to reincarnate him as a mortal human and give him a second chance to forestall final judgment."

Eyes widening, Z winced. "You spoke to Father?"

A lump of dread forming in my throat, I dropped my chin to my chest. "I did. He actually invited me home."

Silence.

Then, a gruff whisper. "I take it you didn't rush home to pack."

Despite being terrified of the hurt I might see written across his features—hurt that *I* caused—I forced myself to meet his gaze. "Knowing who and what Lucifer is, I can't leave him here alone. I don't know what kind of darkness may come along and try to corrupt him, Z. Even if it means watching from a distance, I just need to know that he's safe."

"Are you still in love with him?" Arms folded across his chest, Z's tone was soft and cautious with the faintest tremble of fear snaking through it.

My answer came without an ounce of hesitation. "No, I'm not. I will always have love for him because we shared too many experiences for me to claim otherwise. But, knowing the lies and deceptions he's capable of, I realize what I thought was there never really was. In the romantic sense, I feel nothing for him. Not anymore."

"What does that mean for us?" Lips pressed together in a thin line, Z glanced around at his beloved bar. "For all of this?"

Needing something to do with my jittery hands, I unfastened my shroud and placed the wad of heavy-knit fabric on the countertop. "That part is up to you. I'm staying here and continuing my work as a reaper. I won't lie. I want you by my side every step of the way. Still, knowing I'm here to help *him*, I would understand if you didn't want to be a part of that. Don't get me wrong, it would hurt like hell and would undoubtedly send me into a self-destructive spiral the likes of which the world has never seen. But… yeah, I'd get it."

Ezekiel grabbed the towel draped over his shoulder and wiped off a moisture ring left by Jophiel's glass. "What would you do if I left? Where would you go?"

Thinking about a life without him made my stomach twist and throat tighten. Even I heard how my voice cracked with emotion. "I would have to close the bar. Then, I would embrace the peripatetic lifestyle of a true reaper and spend my days traveling from one harvested soul to the next. A-hole would hate it. She loves her materialistic existence. But if I made sure her one night a year as human was an extravaganza of debauchery, she might bite and claw me slightly less."

Attention focused on the bar top, Ezekiel said nothing as he continued to scrub and polish the length of it.

I gave him a minute—which dragged on for an eternity—to digest everything I laid out before him.

Still, he stayed silent.

Shifting my weight from one foot to the other, I hunted for some straw of patience to cling to.

Heart hammering against my ribs.

Palms sweaty.

Slightly nauseous.

Yeah, any patience I possessed had left the building, jumped in a cab, and fled for the border.

"Okay, I need you to say *something* here, Z. Tell me you'll stay. Scream at me to fuck off. Literally just make words of any kind come out of your mouth."

Gripping the towel tight, his arm stilled. Yet his gaze remained locked on the countertop.

A lead weight sank in my gut.

Icy finality seeped into my veins.

Chin dropping to my chest, I nodded in the bitter acceptance that sometimes silence said more than a shout.

How to move on past that moment, I had no idea. Did I go upstairs and wait for him to clear out his things? Try again to tell him how much he meant to me? Or watch as everything and everyone I cared for tumbled out of my life like ash on a tumultuous gust?

While I was locked in that search for my next step, Ezekiel tossed the towel aside and rounded the bar with slow, measured steps. Catching my hands in his, he swung them back and forth, lightly tapping the knuckles of my index fingers together with each swing.

I peered up at him, finding no trace of answers as to what was going on in his beautiful mind. Wetting my suddenly parched lips, I breathed his name in a desperate search for clarity. "Ezekiel?"

"I do have one thing to say." His voice was a tranquil spring in the middle of an arid desert. A soothing breeze on a scorching day.

"To say I'm eagerly listening would be a vast understatement."

Finally, he glanced my way from under his lashes. One brow lifted, his lips tugged to the side in a sexy smolder. "Are you the Pi symbol? Because I want a love with you that's irrational and endless."

An abrupt bark of laughter escaped me, only to be chased away by the sizzling intensity of his stare. "Is that... really what you want?"

Stepping closer, the tips of his fingers brushed my skin as they curved around the back of my neck. With the pad of his thumb he traced my bottom lip. "The way I see it, there's only one thing more certain than Death and Taxes... and that's you and me."

Heart made whole by his words, I twined my arms around his waist and claimed his lips with mine. For this Angel of Death, Ezekiel was the light that kept the darkness at bay. Now, eternity stretched out before us. Whatever evil came our way, whatever obstacles the future held, as long as we were together... we were ready.

ABOUT THE AUTHOR

Stacey Rourke is the award-winning author of works that span genres. She lives in Florida with her husband, two beautiful daughters, and two spoiled rotten dogs. She loves to travel, is obsessed with all things Disney, and considers herself blessed to make a career out of talking to the imaginary people that live in her head.

Connect with her at:

www.staceyrourke.com
Facebook at www.facebook.com/staceyrourkeauthor
Amazon Author Page: http://amzn.to/2I8FlbH
or on Twitter or Instagram @rourkewrites

Other titles by Stacey Rourke:

The Gryphon Series

The Conduit
Embrace
Sacrifice
Ascension

The Legends Saga

Crane
Raven
Steam

Reel Romance

Adapted for Film
Turn Tables

TS901 Chronicles

Co-written with Tish Thawer
TS901: Anomaly
TS901: Dominion

Veiled Series

Veiled
Vlad
Vendetta

The Journals of Octavia Hollows

Wake the Dead
Dead Man's Hand
Caught Dead
Drop Dead Gorgeous
Dead Ringer
Dead as a Doornail

The Unfortunate Soul Chronicles

Rise of the Sea Witch
Entombed in Glass
Pursuing Madness

The Archive of the Five

The Apocalypse Five
Coming Soon: Rogue Five
Coming Soon: Freedom Five

Fear the Reaper

Reaper vs. Ripper
Reaping a Pain in the Axe
Reaping Rasputin
The Devil You Reap

www.ingramcontent.com/pod-product-compliance
Lightning Source LLC
Chambersburg PA
CBHW021019160726
47994CB00006B/2572